About the Author

Amanda was born in 1976 and grew up in Ballinteer, a suburb of Dublin. She studied Marketing, Advertising and Public Relations at Dublin Business School and worked for several years in marketing and subsequently as P.A. to the chairman at Nissan Ireland. Amanda is also a qualified Montessori teacher and SNA. In 2009, Amanda gave up work to take care of her son Tadhg on a full time basis, after he was diagnosed with cerebral palsy and global developmental delay, at the age of 10 months. Amanda currently lives in Newbridge, Co. Kildare, with her husband Greg and three children, Emily, Tadhg and Dylan.

Dedication

In memory of Mum

Amanda Kehoe

TJ

AND

HIS WHEELABLE CHAIR

AUSTIN MACAULEY
PUBLISHERS LTD.

ISBN 9781786123992 (Paperback)
ISBN 9781786124005 (Hardback)
ISBN 9781786124012 (eBook)

www.austinmacauley.com

First Published (2016)
Austin Macauley Publishers Ltd.
25 Canada Square
Canary Wharf
London
E14 5LQ

Printed and bound in Great Britain

Acknowledgments

I would like to sincerely thank everyone at Austin Macauley for bringing my book to fruition and for their belief in me as a new author. Thanks to all my family and friends who encouraged me to get this book published. A special thanks to all my friends in Nissan Ireland and also to Denis, Vanessa, Sinead, Ashling & Glen, Jeanne, Maria, Sarah, Rachel and Vicky – (thanks for the use of the laptop to help write my book!) – I feel blessed to have such amazing and supportive people in my life.

A special thanks to my sister Tara and her husband Mark and their children, Jack, Beth and Ryan. Also, my good friend Zyna, for your unwavering support and kindness, and for your constant positivity and encouragement - Tadhg is a very lucky boy to have such special people in his life, as am I.

I would like to thank NICE, Centre for Movement Disorders in Birmingham, who have helped Tadhg become more independent and have helped him develop both physically and intellectually – amazing people! I would also like to thank Emma, Martyn and Sid who are the best hosts in Birmingham! Thank you for providing a wonderful place for us to stay on our many trips to the U.K.

Finally, to my husband Greg and our three beautiful children, Emily, Tadhg and Dylan who are my constant inspiration – I love you all so much! Tadhg, thank you for inspiring me every single day and for teaching me about a whole new wonderful world.

This is a story all about me,
and how I do things a little differently,
some days I see people look and stare,
and this can be a little hard for me to bear.
So if you would like to ask about me,
come on over, please feel free.

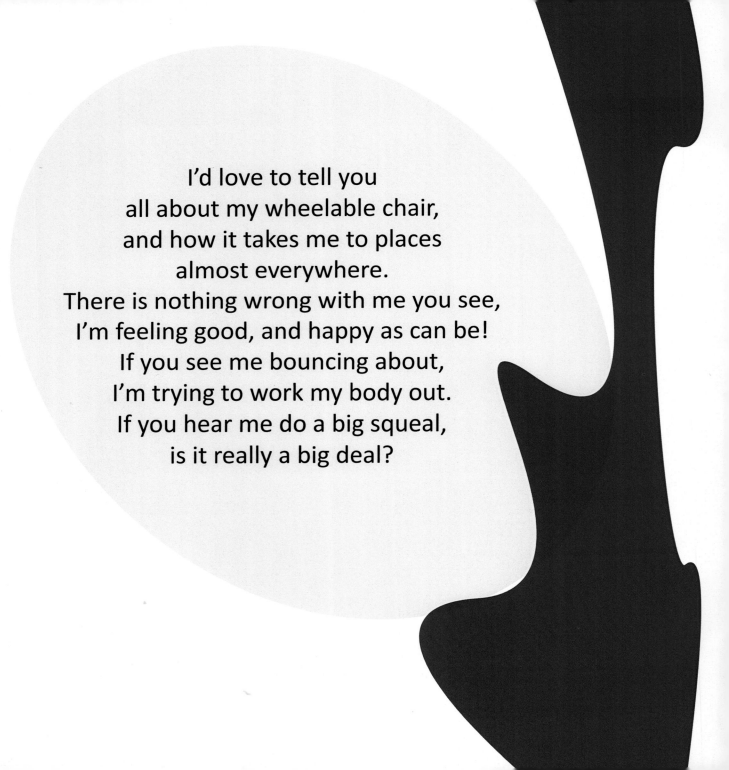

I'd love to tell you
all about my wheelable chair,
and how it takes me to places
almost everywhere.
There is nothing wrong with me you see,
I'm feeling good, and happy as can be!
If you see me bouncing about,
I'm trying to work my body out.
If you hear me do a big squeal,
is it really a big deal?

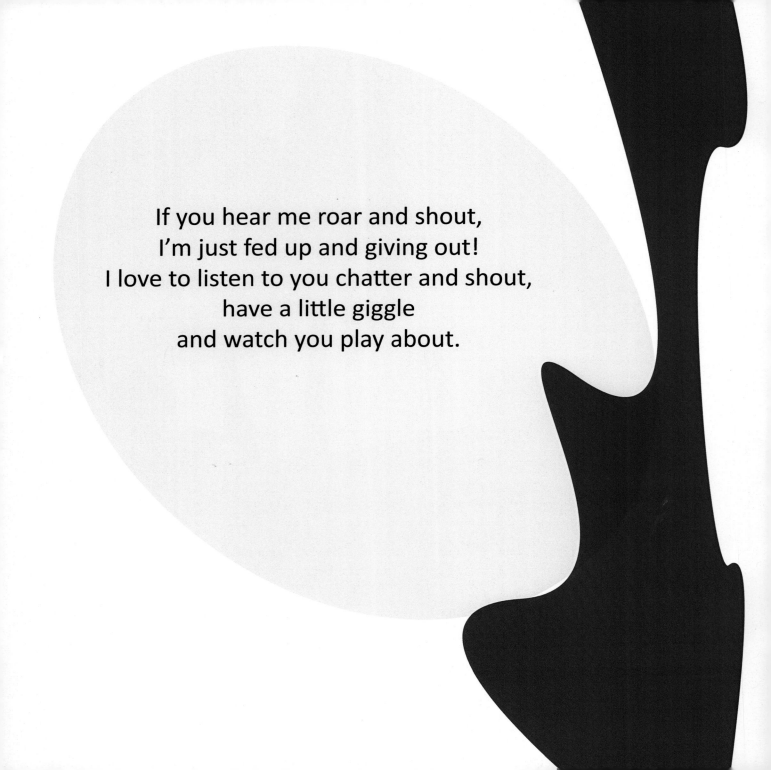

If you hear me roar and shout,
I'm just fed up and giving out!
I love to listen to you chatter and shout,
have a little giggle
and watch you play about.

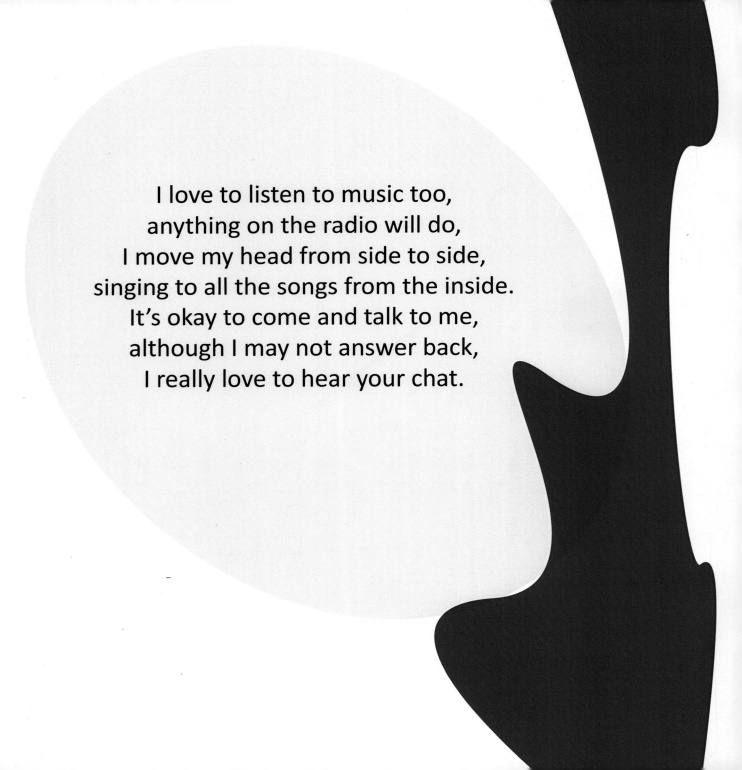

I love to listen to music too,
anything on the radio will do,
I move my head from side to side,
singing to all the songs from the inside.
It's okay to come and talk to me,
although I may not answer back,
I really love to hear your chat.

These are some of the things
that I love to do,
swimming, playing
and horse riding too!
I love to go to the swimming pool,
where I splash about and feel so cool.
I can kick my legs ever so fast,
all you will see is me whizzing past!

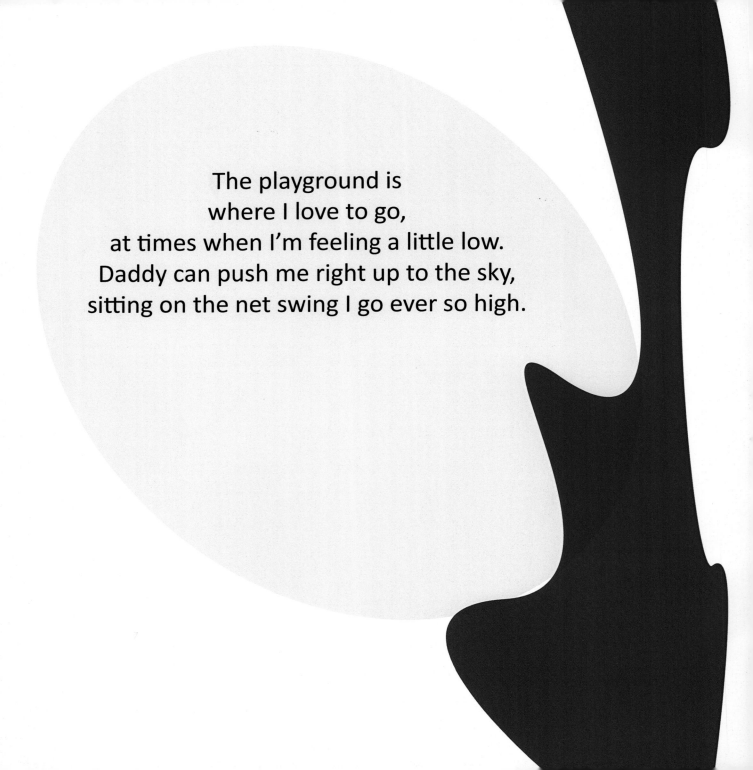

The playground is
where I love to go,
at times when I'm feeling a little low.
Daddy can push me right up to the sky,
sitting on the net swing I go ever so high.

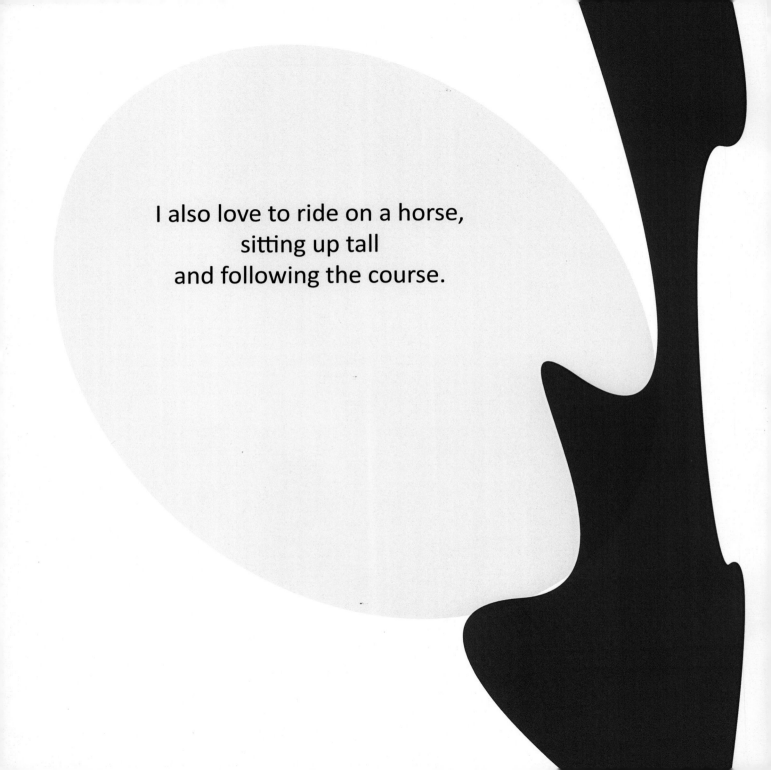

I also love to ride on a horse,
sitting up tall
and following the course.

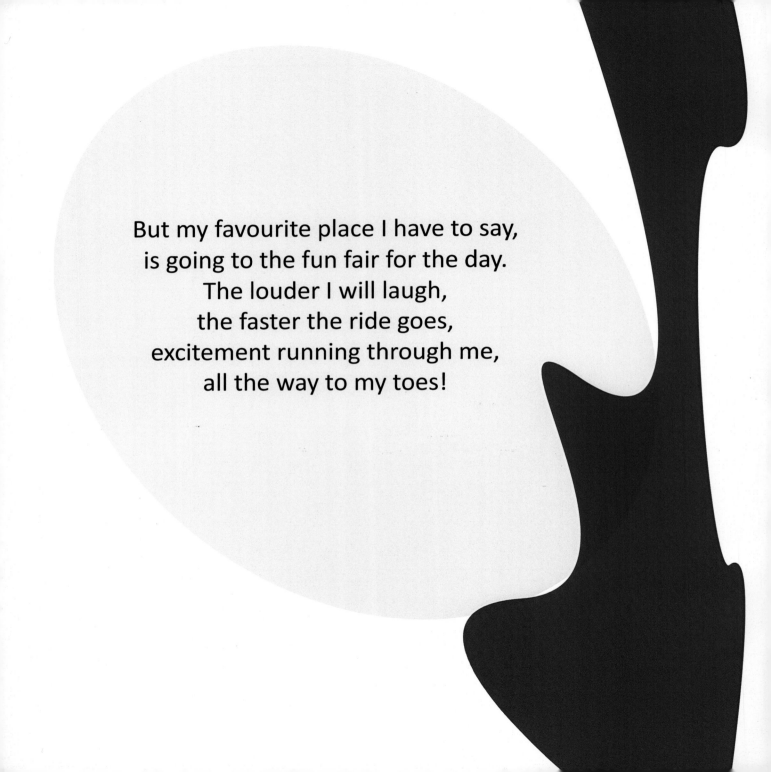

But my favourite place I have to say,
is going to the fun fair for the day.
The louder I will laugh,
the faster the ride goes,
excitement running through me,
all the way to my toes!

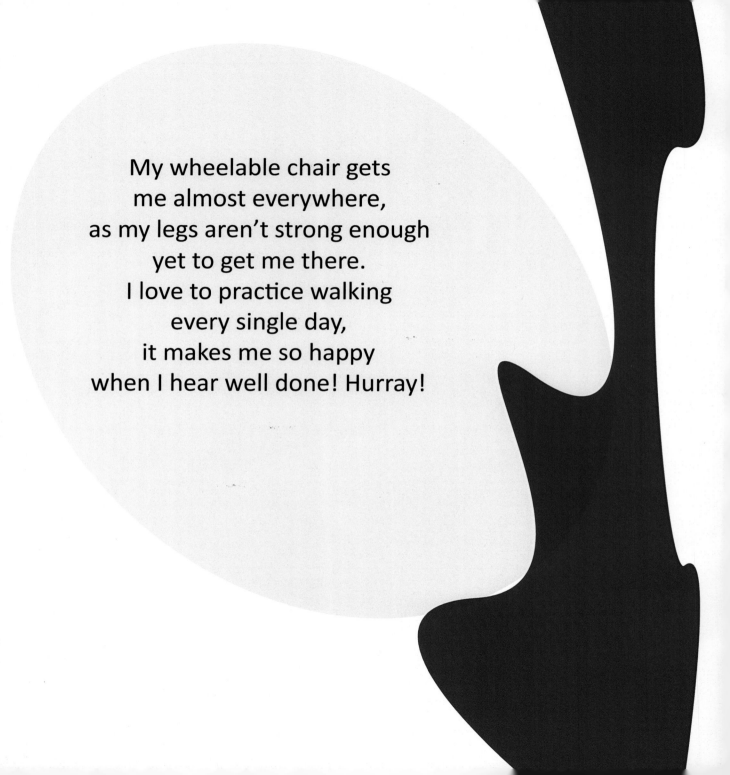

My wheelable chair gets
me almost everywhere,
as my legs aren't strong enough
yet to get me there.
I love to practice walking
every single day,
it makes me so happy
when I hear well done! Hurray!

When it's time to go to bed,
I love to just sit up instead,
you will hear me laugh,
you will hear me shout,
until I hear Mammy say,
"What's this all about?"
I then lie down to go to sleep,
pull up my covers
and I don't make a peep!

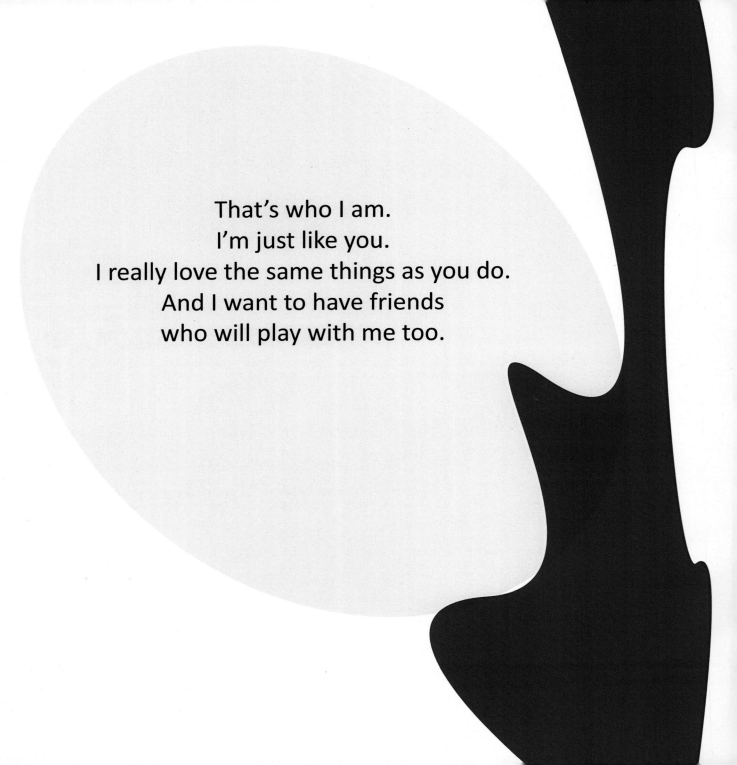

That's who I am.
I'm just like you.
I really love the same things as you do.
And I want to have friends
who will play with me too.

There is nothing wrong with me you see,
I'm feeling good, and I love being me!
If you see me bouncing about,
I'm trying to work my body out.
If you hear me do a big squeal,
is it really a big deal?
If you hear me roar and shout,
I'm just fed up and giving out!"

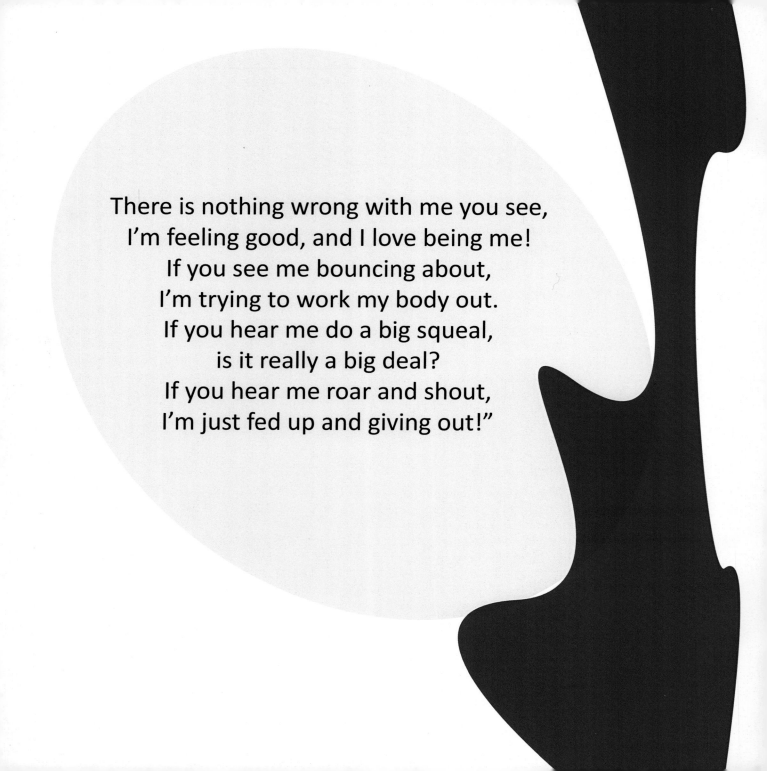

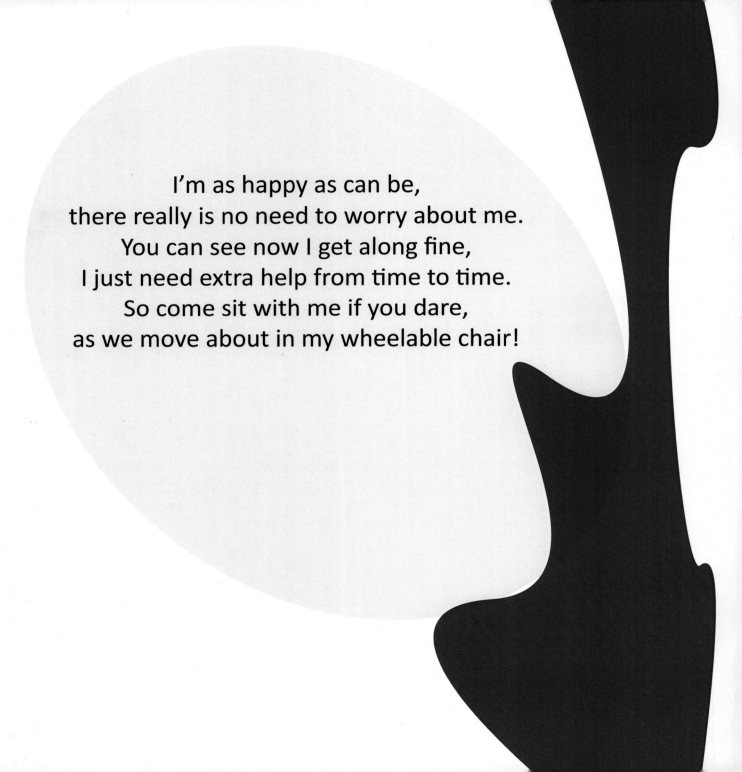

I'm as happy as can be,
there really is no need to worry about me.
You can see now I get along fine,
I just need extra help from time to time.
So come sit with me if you dare,
as we move about in my wheelable chair!

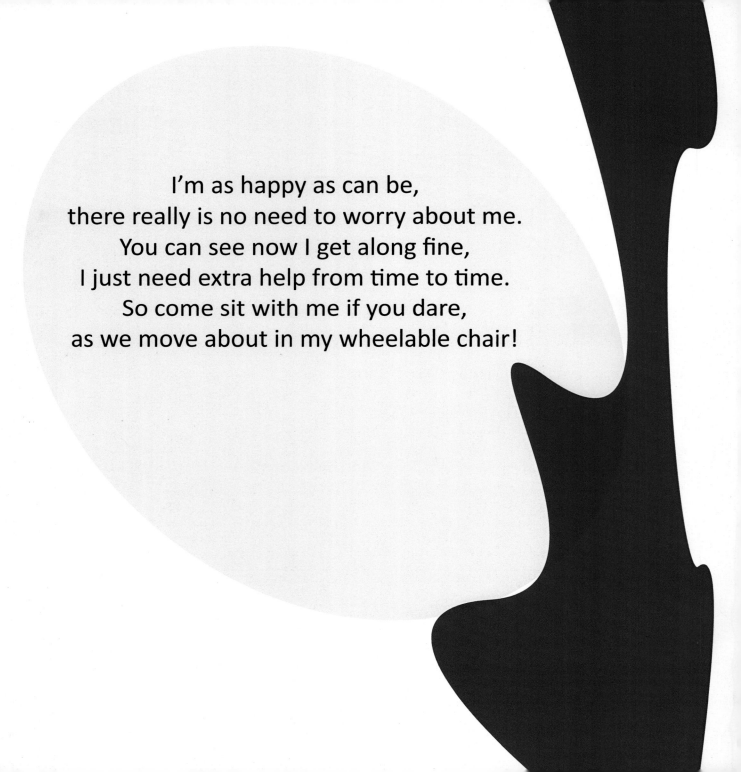

I'm as happy as can be,
there really is no need to worry about me.
You can see now I get along fine,
I just need extra help from time to time.
So come sit with me if you dare,
as we move about in my wheelable chair!